Kelpie Chaos

First published 2024 by FREMANTLE PRESS

Fremantle Press Inc. trading as Fremantle Press
PO Box 158, North Fremantle, Western Australia, 6159
fremantlepress.com.au

Cover illustration and design by Rebecca Mills.
Printed and bound in Australia by Griffin Press.

 A catalogue record for this
book is available from the
National Library of Australia

ISBN: 9781760993856 (paperback)
ISBN: 9781760993863 (ebook)

Publication of this title was assisted by the State Government through
the Department of Local Government, Sport and Cultural Industries.

Fremantle Press respectfully acknowledges the Whadjuk people of the
Noongar nation as the Traditional Owners and Custodians of the land
where we work in Walyalup.

Kelpie Chaos

Deb Fitzpatrick

 FREMANTLE PRESS

For Louie, and all the love that he brings.

Home is where the dog is

When Max ran up the street to our place one night just before dinner, I knew from the sound of his voice that something was up.

'Eli!' he called out, even before his feet hit the porch.

I swung the front door wide open.

'Eli,' Max puffed, 'There's a puppy —'

'Where?' I asked, looking over his shoulder.

'No, no,' he said, 'Not here. Not here.' He sucked in a breath.

'Come in, Max,' Dad said. 'Grab a seat.'

Max sat down at the counter.

I hopped up on the stool next to him. 'What's happened?'

Max took a second, then the story came out in a big gush.

Max's parents' friend's uncle's second cousin — or something like that — owned a farm and kept working dogs. One of the dogs had just had pups and the family had more animals than they could manage. They were keeping one, and giving away the others. But there was one puppy left that they couldn't find a home for.

'And —' said Max.

'And?' I said.

'*And*, they're going to take him to the pound if they haven't found a home for him by the end of the week.'

'The pound … that's okay, isn't it? Isn't that where people looking for dogs go? It's like a rescue shelter, right?'

'Yeah, but … Mum says not all of the animals find new owners.'

'What happens then?' I asked.

Max looked at Dad. Dad looked down at his Ugg boots.

'Dad?' I said. 'What happens then?'

Max gnawed on a fingernail.

Dad finally said, 'If they're not adopted after a while, Eli, well, they have to be put down.'

I felt my face fall. 'You mean … put to sleep?'

Dad nodded.

'Oh. That's horrible.'

'Mum said they — the farmer people — have tried really hard to find homes for the puppies,' Max explained. 'They've asked all around town and put ads up and everything, but they just can't find anyone to take the last one.

'And Dad said we can't take on any more pets. The rabbit had babies last week; eight bunnies. We weren't expecting that. Dad said he was *sure* it was a boy.

'*So*,' Max finished up, 'you don't know anyone who's looking for a puppy, do you?'

The farm was a long drive from the city. We turned off the main road at a sign that said Sheedon Lot 417. Our car bumped and jiggled along the dirt track into the farm.

We came to a gate with a sign on it.

PLEASE CLOSE THE GATE

'I'll get it!' I scrambled out of the car. There was a fat chain securing the gate, and it latched onto a big bolt on the other side. I carefully unhooked the chain, drew it through the hand slot and swung the gate wide open so Dad could drive through. Then I closed it, just like the sign said, and hopped back in the car.

'Good job, mate,' said Dad.

Lexie made a face at me. But I didn't care. Nothing could ruin today.

Our old dog, Schnoozle, died a year ago. Mum and Dad got him before I was even born. The house seemed weird and empty without him. At night it was super quiet without the sound of him padding around on the floorboards.

Dad, me and Lexie all wanted to get another dog fairly quickly but Mum said she needed more time.

'I don't want to forget Schnoozle,' she said.

I hugged her. I knew what she meant.

Finally, a few months ago, Mum announced she was ready for another pooch. 'A home is no place without a dog,' she said.

Then Max ran up the street to our place, and now we were finally getting our puppy!

We kept driving until we saw a big shed with a green tractor parked next to it. They had a quad bike and a trail bike as well.

'Phwoar.' Mum turned around and grinned at us. '*They* look fun.'

'I'd love to have a go on that quad bike,' Lexie said.

'And *I'd* love to have a go on the motorbike,' Dad said.

'That leaves us with the tractor, Eli,' Mum laughed. 'You happy to drive?'

'Sounds good to me!' I smiled back at her in the side mirror.

'I wonder what this pup's going to be like,' Mum said. 'The farmer — Rob —'

'Max's parents' friend's uncle's second cousin,' Dad added helpfully.

Mum laughed again. 'Yep, him. Well, Rob said there were four puppies in the litter. Rob's keeping one, two have been adopted by families nearby, and we're taking the last one.'

Dad looked at her. 'I hope that doesn't mean it's the runt.'

'Dad!' said Lexie. 'That's mean!'

'Well, it's a real thing you know, in nature — most litters have a runt. The weakest, smallest baby.'

'Like Eli, you mean?'

I rolled my eyes and poked out my tongue.

'Lexie,' Mum warned. Dad tried not to laugh.

'Rob said to keep going past the sheds until we reach the house.' Mum was reading from her phone. 'There's a big bougainvillea out the front, apparently.'

We kept crawling along the track, gravel crunching beneath our tyres. I looked out the rear windscreen. A cloud of dust hung in the air behind us.

Dad took a bend and Lexie squealed, 'There it is!'

Dogs barked and ran towards our car. One was a beautiful black-and-tan kelpie.

'That's enough.' A man wearing Blundstone boots and work clothes came out. He smiled and waited as Dad parked the car next to a huge hedge of bright pink flowers.

We jumped out. While the adults were talking the kelpie trotted over to us, tail sweeping from side to side.

'Awww,' Lexie said, 'He's beautiful.'

I put my hand out for him to sniff and said, 'Hello, fella.'

'That's a female, actually,' said the farmer to us. 'That's your pup's mum.'

'Oh, really?' Mum came over for a pat. 'She's lovely.'

Rob laughed. 'Yeah. We weren't too happy when we

realised she was pregnant. We hadn't wanted any more dogs. But the neighbour's dog seems to have paid her a visit or two, and, hey presto, we found ourselves with a litter of puppies.'

Dad nodded to us. 'And that's how it happens, kids.'

'D-a-a-d,' groaned Lexie. 'Please!'

'We're really glad you came on board.' Rob lowered his voice but I still heard him: 'We didn't want to have to take him to the pound. We'd run out of options.'

'Well, it works for us, too,' Dad said. 'I think it's what we could call a win-win.'

'Absolutely,' Mum nodded. 'What breed is the father?'

'He's an Australian shepherd. They're quite big with a thick coat. Some folk reckon they're a bit sooky.' He laughed again. 'They call them Velcro dogs, 'cos they always stick close to you.'

Dad started to look worried.

'But they're really affectionate. Great family dogs.'

Mum let out a breath and smiled at us. 'Oh. Well. That sounds good, doesn't it? Just what we're looking for.'

'And mixed with the kelpie,' Rob went on, 'they're hard workers. Smart as. Great working dogs, especially with sheep. Really good herders.'

Dad started to look worried again, but I stood a bit taller. Our dog was going to be great!

Rob looked at me and Lexie. 'Do you want to meet him? Your pup?'

'Yes!'

'He's right over here. Let's go.'

Shiny-eyed, floppy-eared, jet-black cuteness

Rob took us into a big shed next to the house, where the dogs lived.

Dad looked around. 'So they don't live in the house with you?'

'No, our dogs are working dogs,' Rob explained. 'They're not pets. They're happy in here.'

Two puppies came bounding over to us. Lexie and I dropped to our knees to play with them. One was black with tan patches, just like its mum. The other was pure black, and fluffy, with a white flame on its chest.

'So the black-and-tan girl is the one we're keeping to train up and work on the farm,' Rob said, 'and this other little fella is your new pup. He's eleven weeks old.'

The shiny-eyed, floppy-eared, big-pawed, jet-black

thing was so cute that we all made embarrassing love-noises. The furry bundle squiggled around as we patted him, our hands on his soft fur.

He was the newest member of our family!

Mum's eyes shone. 'He is adorable. I'm so glad Max told us about him.'

Dad couldn't stop smiling as he rubbed the pup's soft black cheeks.

Lexie kept saying, 'Awwww,' as she watched him.

I sat down on the ground, cross-legged, calling him over for a cuddle. His little body bulleted into my lap and sat still for a couple of moments. From my lap he looked up at Mum, Dad and Lexie. I put my hands around him and felt the size of him, and his warmth.

'Well, there you go,' said Rob, giving me a nod. 'Looks like he knows who's boss.'

Mum smiled. 'He zoomed right over to you, didn't he?'

Dad tilted his head at her and paused a moment before saying, 'Name idea?'

'Hmmm?'

'Zoom,' Dad said. 'For our little Speedy Gonzales here.'

'Well, he is pretty zoomy, that's for sure,' she agreed.

Lexie quietly said, 'Hey Zoom. Zoomy Zoom.'

I stroked his smooth head. He playfully put his mouth over my wrist and pressed down.

'Yow!! Sharp teeth!'

'Aaah, yes, those are his baby teeth,' said Rob. 'You'd think they'd be nice and gentle, but those things are razor sharp. You definitely need to be careful.'

I took my hand out of his mouth and rubbed it. Ouch!

'What we do,' Rob said, squatting next to me, 'is give him something he's allowed to chew on. Like this.' He produced a rubbery puppy bone. 'This toy is pretty well indestructible. You can take this one with you; it's his favourite.'

I gave our puppy a big squeeze. He jumped forward and licked my ears with his soft pink tongue, making me giggle.

'All right, let's get out of your hair,' said Dad to Rob. 'Pop him in the car, kids.'

'You'll probably find he sleeps most of the way,' Rob said. 'He's still a young 'un and needs his naps.'

We put our puppy in the laundry basket we'd brought, with soft blankets all around him, and he disappeared into his puppy nest. Lexie and I grinned at one another and then at him. We both had a hand in the basket, stroking him. His ears felt like pieces of velvet from Granny's sewing box.

'He's like our own soft toy!' I said, feeling a big glow of love inside.

We waved our goodbyes and Dad bumped back down the track.

'They'll probably miss him, don't you think?' Mum said to no one in particular. 'Having cared for him since he was born. It must be hard to give young pups away, even if you know you can't keep them.'

She turned around in her seat to see what the puppy was up to in the back.

His eyes were glazing over and his eyelids were sliding down. And lifting up. And dropping down again.

'He's falling asleep,' Mum whispered. 'Just like Rob said he would.'

I held the tip of his tail in my hand. 'He's not very zoomy now,' I said with a grin.

'All that zoominess before is probably why he's so tired now,' said Dad. 'Everyone — every*thing* — needs a break from time to time, even a high-energy pup like this.'

I turned around to see the disappearing farm. There was another cloud of dust between our car and Rob's house and sheds.

I rubbed the hairy tip of Zoom's tail. I hoped he was happy to be coming home with us. It was definitely better than going to the pound, that's for sure.

My sister is right (for once)

'So, is it agreed?' Mum asked at dinner that night. 'Our little furry one's name is Zoom?'

We looked at each other.

'Bruce?' Dad offered, reaching for another pickle.

'Goose?' Mum replied.

'That'll get confusing,' said Dad.

'Prince?'

'Biscuit?'

'Ninja?'

Lexie rolled her eyes at me.

'Well it's better than *Prince*!'

Mum changed tack. 'Mister Wigglebottom? Snoopy?'

There was a pause then, so I said what I'd been thinking: 'He already *is* Zoom, to me. I can't get the name out of my head, ever since Dad said it.'

'Me too,' Lexie said.

'That's it, then,' said Dad.

'At least it's original,' laughed Mum.

We looked at him. He was sitting on the mat next to the door that goes out into our garden. He knew we were talking about him. Every few seconds he'd get up on his oversized paws and wag his tail, looking at us. Then he'd plop his bottom back down on the mat.

'Good boy, Zoom,' said Dad. 'Sit.'

'He is sitting,' said Lexie.

'I know. I was listening to a dog trainer on the radio the other day, and he explained that that's how you train them: you wait for them to do the thing you want them to do and then give it a name — like "sit" or "lie down" or whatever. You say that word and praise the dog while they're doing it. That's how they learn to associate the word with the action.'

'Oh ... so then, when you say "sit" later on, they know what that is?' Mum said.

'Exactly.'

'That's amazing!'

'That's what I thought. This guy knew his stuff. Made it sound so easy.'

'Zoom,' I called, and reached out my hand. But he

was staring at a fly, his head to one side, ears pointing like wizard hats. With every buzzy movement our puppy's eyes widened. The fly whizzed right past his face. He snapped at it, but missed. That was it; the challenge was on! Zoom's feet slipped on our wooden floorboards as he tried to get close to it. The fly landed on the ground, next to one of the stools. Zoom put out his paw, quite gently, almost like he wanted to play. But the fly took off, and this time our puppy leapt and — SNAP! — did the job on him.

'Ha ha! Nice work, buddy,' said Dad.

'Eww, did he swallow that?' Lexie put her fork down.

'That'll be helpful in summer,' said Mum. 'We need a snappy-jawed fly-catcher around the place.'

'You'll have to get Max over to meet, him, Eli,' said Dad. 'He'll be really happy with how things worked out, I'm sure.'

I nodded, but chewed my lip. 'I still …'

'What, love?'

'Well … Schnoozle. I don't want to … forget about him,' I said.

Mum's hand snaked across the table to mine. 'No, Eli. You don't need to. You can love them both — we all can.'

Dad pulled the stubble on his chin. 'You don't need to feel bad about loving Zoom, mate. We have a lot of room in our hearts, you know.'

I nodded and took in a breath. I did love Schnoozle. He was a beautiful dog. He was nearly fifteen years old when he died.

'Schnoozle knew we loved him,' Lexie said. 'Every time we took him for a walk or played tug-of-war with him, he knew. That's what I think, anyway.'

I looked at my sister. She was right (for once). Schnoozle was loved, and he knew it. And now we were falling in love with Zoom, and maybe that was okay.

I sat up. 'Where will he sleep?'

Mum and Dad exchanged a glance.

'We're going to try him outside, next to the back door,' Dad said. 'Just at night, seeing he's used to sleeping outside at the farm.'

'But that was in a shed, Dad,' Lexie's brow furrowed.

'I know, but let's see how it goes. I've set up a box for him undercover, so he won't get wet if it rains or anything. There's lots of snuggly blankets in the box. And he can come inside during the day.'

'Schnoozle slept inside at night,' Lexie said, eyes flaring.

'Yes, that's true,' said Mum. 'But if he— if Zoom's

used to it, then it should be okay. He's spent his whole life so far sleeping apart from his humans, so why change now? And this way there won't be any … accidents.'

'There *were* other dogs with him in the shed at the farm, though, weren't there?' Dad said. 'So he wasn't alone out there.'

Mum looked at him and half laughed. 'Don't go changing your mind on me now. We have to begin as we mean to continue.'

Then I remembered! 'Hey, he *will* have company — Snow and Red will be out there with him!'

Lexie sat up. 'How could we forget about the guineas?' she cried. 'He might try to *eat* them.'

'No, no. It's okay,' said Dad. 'We'll get out their old hutch, and put them in there while they all get used to each other.'

Mum nodded. 'Thank goodness we kept that hutch. I'll give it a sweep out and perhaps you kids can get some newspapers to line the bottom? We don't have any straw left so maybe we should tear up lots of strips of paper so they can snuggle down at night till we get some more.'

I hopped up. We'd had Snow and Red since they were tiny fluffball babies. Now they were full-size and

Red even had a couple of dreadlocks in his long hair.

'Catching them will be the thing,' said Dad. 'Now they're free-range they're like wild warriors of the garden. They don't seem to want to come too close anymore.'

'They love their freedom,' said Lexie, 'after all those years in the boring hutch.'

It was true. When Schnoozle died, we'd decided to let them have the run of the garden. The hutch looked so small. Just a box. Even with lots of fresh straw in it, we thought their lives must be super boring. When we let them out, they seemed to love it, scampering around on the lawn, hiding among the ferns, and drinking from Schnoozle's old water bowl. After a while they seemed to recognise the sound of the screen door opening, and they'd come out, *kwee-kwee-kwee!*, calling for food.

So now we sprinkle all our vegetable and fruit peelings out there. They bound over, Red's long hair flopping around his face, and Snow with his shorter, sleek black-and-white coat, and munch through all our offerings.

They were not going to enjoy being back in the hutch.

'Just for the first few days,' Mum said, giving me a

shoulder-squeeze. 'Until they get used to Zoom.'

'And *he* learns that he's not allowed to *eat* them,' Lexie said.

'So, just checking,' Dad said, 'we're still sticking with Plan A?'

Mum looked at him.

'Plan A: Zoom sleeps outside.'

'Ah, yes,' Mum said. 'I think so, don't you? The guineas will be in their hutch, safe and sound, and Zoom will be in his box beside them. He'll probably sense that's where the animals sleep. So yes, Plan A.'

In the middle of the night I saw light coming under my bedroom door. I opened it to see Mum, sitting on the kitchen floor, cuddling Zoom. He was licking her neck.

She looked at me guiltily. 'He was whining at the door. I thought he'd wake everyone, the little blighter!'

I went over to join them. Zoom's body was warm and wiggly in my arms and filled me with that fizzing glowy feeling. I grinned, at nothing in particular.

'He's gorgeous, isn't he,' whispered Mum, stroking his ears.

I brought him close to my face and buried my nose in his fur. I already loved him so much!

Who knew dogs have hobbies?

Over the next few months we got to know Zoom and he got to know us. He changed from tiny and cute and easy to pick up in one hand, to lanky and foxy with ears that looked way too big for his head.

'I really hope his ears don't grow any more,' I said.

'They don't look quite right on his head, do they?' said Mum.

'What do you mean?'

'Well, what *you* meant, I think!'

'But … he's still handsome, isn't he?'

'Oh yes,' she said. 'Very.'

I learnt that:

  • Zoom is the world's best dog (but I still love Schnoozle, too).

  • Zoom steals Lexie's toast when she's not looking.

• Zoom loves having his tummy scratched.

• Zoom rolls onto his back when we're passing him in the hope we'll stop to give him a tummy-scratch.

• Zoom has a hobby: collecting our socks.

Who knew that dogs had hobbies? I mean, I knew they loved to dig. Zoom had dug a few holes in the lawn, which made Dad do deep-breathing before giving him a lecture. I'm not sure Zoom understood everything Dad said, but by the look on his little face, he tried. Then Zoom lay down at the other end of the lawn and put his head on his paws and watched while Dad filled in the holes with the shovel.

We first realised Zoom had a hobby when we discovered about six different odd socks on his bed. (Plan A didn't last long — now his bed's a huge cushion inside next to the fireplace.)

Mum snatched up the socks, about to be cross, then examined them and said, 'He hasn't chewed any of these. That's weird.' She turned them inside out to be sure. 'And good. We don't need to have a sock-chewer in the house. It's hard enough to keep all these growing feet in socks as it is!'

'He just collects them, then,' Lexie said, giggling. 'You funny boy, Zoom.' She held up a white ankle sock with a light blue heel. 'This one's mine! Doesn't it stink from netball today?'

Zoom swished his tail from side to side. He looked really proud of himself.

From then on, whenever someone was looking for socks, Mum would say, 'Check the laundry basket.' Then she'd lower her voice in mock grumpiness and say, 'And check Zoom's bed.'

Zoom knew he wasn't allowed on the couches or on any of our beds, except when we invited him up. Dad said it was all about making sure he knew who was the top dog.

'When *we* invite him up on the couch, that's quite different from him just jumping up whenever he wants,' Dad said. 'Apparently,' he tapped the cover of a book called *Training Your Puppy for Life*, 'dogs associate height with status. So, when they get up on the couch or the bed, they're trying to assert themselves.'

'Oh for goodness sake,' said Mum, pouring herself a

coffee. 'What a load of —'

'Kate!' Dad warned. 'Little ears …'

Mum looked around at us. 'Well. That sounds like pop — pup — psychology to me.'

'Ha ha, very clever.' Dad read from the back cover of the book: 'This guy is "a world-renowned dog trainer with decades of experience training all breeds of dog".'

'Well *good on him*,' Mum grumbled. 'I like it when Zoom gets on the bed with me. Especially when I'm having a nap on the weekend. He's a lovely companion. Furry and soft.'

'I know. But apparently we're making a rod for our own backs by letting him do it whenever he wants,' Dad said.

Zoom was lying on the rug on the floor having a nap during this conversation. Every now and then he'd open one eye, check out what was happening, then close it and nod off again. Eventually he rolled onto his back and stretched. Then he went over to the sofa where Dad was reading his dog training book, and sat right in front of him, really close. Zoom lifted his paw and put it on the edge of the sofa. Mum, Lexie and I were watching.

'Awwww,' said Lexie. 'D-a-d! Don't be mean! Let him up!'

'I'm not being mean, Lexie, I'm being firm. Firm but fair.'

Mum pressed her lips together as Zoom's other paw went up to the edge of the sofa. We were trying not to laugh at Dad's attempts to ignore him.

Zoom pushed his bum off the ground slightly so he was crouched, in a half-up-on-the-sofa, half-on-the-ground position.

'Da-ad,' I laughed. 'What are you going to do?'

'Zoom, down,' Dad said.

Zoom's bottom lowered back to the floor, but his two front paws stayed up on the sofa. He poked his nose under Dad's hand.

'Oh, seriously,' Dad said, rubbing his schnoz. 'You're a kelpie, Zoom, not a lap dog!'

'He still needs cuddles, though,' I said.

Dad sniffed. 'He gets plenty of love from all of us. It doesn't mean he needs to be *on the sofa* as well.'

Right then, Zoom pushed off the ground really gently with his hind legs and crept onto Dad's lap, almost as though Dad might not notice him if he did it softly enough.

'Ohhh,' Mum crooned, and smiled.

Dad laughed and gave in. 'It's impossible not to love you.' He gave him a big scratch and pat and then said, 'Okay, mate, that's enough. Hop down now please, Zoom.'

And Zoom did, just like that.

There was one other thing we learnt about Zoom.

Zoom likes cake.

Cake.

And cake makes him really naughty.

It was my birthday. Max and a bunch of other friends came over after school. Max arrived first and Zoom went straight to his box of toys and picked out the old sock Mum had left in there and padded back over to him for a game of tug-of-war.

'Come on, Zoom, let's see if you can beat Uncle Max,' Max said.

I giggled. 'You're not his uncle.'

'Sort of am,' Max said. 'Godfather.'

Zoom growled in his pretend-fierce way as Max pulled on the other end of that sock and yanked it left and right. When Max let go, Zoom would adjust his grip on the sock and then offer it again to his playmate.

'He won't let me win!' Max said, and eventually let go. 'Alright then Zoom, you're the top doggo, that's for sure.'

Kai and Marley arrived and we went outside to kick the ball. Kai was just climbing back over the fence with the ball when we heard Mum scream, then roar. I'm talking lion stuff.

'ZOOOOOOOOOOOOM!'

The side door flew open and Zoom came out, tail between his legs.

Mum's face was the crossest I've ever seen it.

'What's happened, Mum?'

'The cupcakes,' she said. 'He's got into them!'

We went inside to have a look. The kitchen was a warzone of cake crumbs and patty pans, half-eaten cupcakes and destroyed cupcakes and yet-to-be-eaten cupcakes rolling around on the floor.

Mum's ears may as well have been blasting steam. She was next-level angry.

'There's still a few left,' Max said.

I counted hopefully. 'Yeah, look, Mum, there's enough for us to have one each—' I re-counted, '—If you press those two halves together ...'

Mum gave me a hug. 'Good on you, Eli. You boys

go back outside and play and I'll sort this mess out and bring you some birthday cupcakes. At least we know Zoom hasn't got into the corn chips and dip!'

So now we have a new rule: The kitchen is a Zoom-Free Zone.

And if there's ever cake around, it gets put away. Just in case.

After school when I'm on my bed reading graphic novels and drawing, I call Zoom over and invite him up next to me. He sits right on top of me sometimes, no matter how uncomfortable that is for both of us, and it makes me laugh. I talk to him and scratch all the bits I know he likes (his chest is his favourite spot, where his white fur-flame is, and he seems to enjoy a good scratching under his collar). Then, when I'm done, I pat my hand on the bit of my doona that's free of books and markers. 'Here, boy,' I say. 'Over here.'

Zoom turns around and around and around on the spot before he finally lies down, in just the right position. He curls up like a furry doughnut.

I love it when he sleeps on my bed. It feels like I

have a friend hanging out with me in my room. I put one of my socks next to his nose for when he wakes.

If I have a crumb of cake left from afternoon tea, I put it there too. On the sock.

Just don't say 'wal–'

Every day we walk Zoom twice.

'Because he's such an active breed,' Dad had said when we first got him, 'we have to commit to that. It will make sure he grows into a happy, healthy dog.'

And boy, does going for a walk make Zoom a happy dog.

It doesn't matter if he is completely asleep, in full furry doughnut mode, if one of us even *whispers* the word 'walk', his head lifts up, he blinks and trots over to us, tail wagging.

'Good grief,' Mum says. 'We're going to have to be very careful about using the "w" word. Look at him! Well, I suppose we can't let him down now.'

'Can I take him, Mum?' I ask.

'I was hoping you were going to say that,' she smiles,

holding her hands up in the air. 'I'm right in the middle of making these and would rather finish, if that's okay.'

I see a plate loaded with Mum's yummy lamb koftas. No broccoli in sight. 'Dinner's looking good,' I grin.

'Just to the park and back, all right?' she says as I pull on my sneakers.

Our local park is a big sports oval just around the block. I'm glad it's close because Zoom pulls a lot on the lead, and I reckon my arm must be getting a bit longer every time I walk him.

We have to cross one road to get there. Zoom's so smart that I don't even have to say 'Sit' now when we wait to cross. He just drops down, head pointing at the big green oval, and waits for me to say, 'Okay.' Then he gets up and yanks me across the road, and doesn't stop yanking until we reach the edge of the park. As soon as he has grass under his paws, he relaxes on the lead.

'Zoom, sit,' I say. He lowers his bum but it doesn't quite touch the ground. 'Zooooooom,' I repeat. He looks at me quickly, as if to say 'What?'

'Sit.'

When he finally does, I lean down and unclick his lead, but keep my hand on his collar. 'Wait,' I say. Again, he looks at me. 'Good boy.' I rub his neck. 'Okay, go play.'

He bolts off to the nearest tree, and starts sniffing

the smells. Then he adds one of his own, in a long noisy stream, right next to the tree trunk. Zoom doesn't cock his leg when he does a wee. Our vet friend told us that not all male dogs lift their leg, especially when they're young. Zoom squats. Which makes it hard sometimes to know if he's doing a wee or a … well, you get the picture.

Then, job done, he sprints for the open grass of the oval. He swivels around to face me and crouches low, waiting for me to throw his ball.

We have one of those ball-chucker things that lets you fling the ball *super far*. Zoom goes bananas, running as fast as he can to get it, snatching the orange squeezy ball in his mouth and looking at me like he's holding the Olympic gold medal for dog-sprints.

A couple of other dogs are here too. They see Zoom and run across the oval to play, but after a quick sniff hello Zoom lies down on the grass and stares at me. He wants the ball. Again.

'Zoom, be friendly — play with the other dogs,' I try. 'Go on.'

'Cute pup,' one of the other dog-walkers says to me, nodding at Zoom.

I grin. 'Thanks.'

'Kelpie?' she asks.

I nod.

'Well, that explains it.' She stops. 'He doesn't want to play with the other dogs — they're just silly creatures as far as he's concerned. Your dog wants to work that ball!'

I look at Zoom. He hasn't moved an inch, despite the other dogs trying to get his attention, coming up close to him, sniffing around his bum. Lots of rude sniffing. And barking. One dog barks right at him, trying to get him to play.

The woman laughs kindly. 'Good luck with that, Spud,' she says to her dog. 'That dog's got work to do.' Then she says to me, 'I tried to get Spud into chasing a ball, but he's just not interested. He only wants to play with other dogs.' She wanders off, calling Spud. 'Have a lovely walk,' she says to me, waving.

'Thank you, you too.'

I lock eyes with Zoom. He lowers himself even further into the grass, his head down on his paws, his back legs in a half-crouch, ready to go. I fling the ball as far as I can and it arcs across the sky. He springs off, catches up with it and snatches it mid-air.

'Good boy!' I call, feeling proud of my smart working dog. Then we do it again. And again, and again. And again. Until eventually, Zoom lies down on the grass, but not in the throw-me-the-ball position. He lies with his tummy on the ground and his head raised up, looking away from me. He's panting, and looking tired and happy.

I go over and sit next to him. 'Good boy, Zoom. You have a rest.' I lie down beside him and we watch clouds.

The sky is changing colour, and there's a coolness in the air.

Some cars pull into the parking bays next to the clubrooms and teenagers get out, pulling up long striped socks and clacking across the carpark in their studded boots. I look at Zoom. 'Footy training. Time to get out of here.'

I click on his lead and give him a big ruffle around the neck. Dad told us The Book said we should praise him whenever we put him on his lead — especially if he doesn't try to scamper off for one last tree-sniff. Or bird-chase. Or chip-munch.

But tonight he seems ready to head home.

'Good boy,' I whisper into his ear. 'Ready for your dinner?' He looks at me with his smart brown eyes. 'Let's go,' I say, grinning.

How to round up lawnmowers and guinea pigs

One morning when I'm getting ready for school, Mum is clipping on Zoom's lead.

'Oh, can I can come too?' I ask.

'That would be fun!' She looks at her watch. 'Yes, I think you have time.'

Zoom pulls us in the direction of the park, ears and nose on high alert. As we hit the lush green carpet I see the gardeners are there and there's a big red ride-on mower trundling over the grass. Mum unclips Zoom's lead and throws him the ball, which he races after and snatches up like a champion.

And then he sees the mower. And he goes *ballistic*. Zoom drops the ball and bolts for the mower, barking.

When he reaches it he runs around and around and around the red machine, barking like it's a giant monster or something!

'Zoom!' I call, and try to whistle.

'Zoom!' Mum calls, louder.

But he completely ignores us. He runs and barks and runs and barks and *will not stop*.

Mum runs towards him, calling so loudly that her voice cracks. She waves her arms and tries everything she can to get Zoom's attention, but he is totally focused on that ride-on mower. He weaves up and down alongside it, barking and barking and barking. It's killing my ears!

Finally, the mower stops moving.

Zoom stops barking.

Mum waves to the driver. 'Zoom!' she calls firmly. 'Come here.' He finally trots over. Mum grabs his collar and puts his lead on. She's frowning, and fumbles with the clip.

'I'm really sorry about that,' I hear her say as she approaches the mower-driver. 'I did not expect him to chase you like that!'

'No worries,' he says, but he's not smiling. He starts up the engine and gets back to work.

I catch up with Mum and Zoom. Mum looks

flustered. 'Goodness me, that was a bit of a debacle.'

'That was bad with the lawnmower, Zoom,' I say, kneeling down next to him. 'You have to come when we call you.'

Mum shakes her head. 'That poor gardener! Well. I won't be letting Zoom off the lead next time I see a mower here. No wonder the gardener was grumpy, having a furry bullet running rings around his machinery. Must be hard trying to mow straight lines with a dog shouting at you.'

She stops to breathe. 'Plus,' she says, looking thoughtful, 'Zoom could get hurt. Those things have sharp cutting blades. You wouldn't want him to get a paw caught ...'

'Yow,' I say, grimacing at the idea. '*No* chasing the mowers, Zoom.' I try a stern voice but then feel bad so I stroke his ears.

'Let's go home,' Mum sighs. 'That's a very short walk for you this morning I'm afraid, Zoom.'

Zoom's tongue is hanging out of his mouth and he's panting.

'Short but ... busy,' I say with a small grin.

'Hmmm,' Mum says. 'Not my idea of a nice morning walk.'

Zoom tries hard to sit still while I get his breakfast together, but his bottom has a bad case of the wiggles. I put a few spoonfuls of kangaroo meat and a scoop of biscuits into his silver bowl. Sometimes Dad cracks an egg on top, or a big blob of natural yoghurt, as a bit of a treat. Zoom follows me outside and sits. His eyes are huge anticipating saucers, waiting for me to put his bowl on the ground. Dad's rule is, Zoom has to wait for us to say 'Okay' before he's allowed to start chowing down. And he really does chow down. Boy does he like his food!

'It's a matter of manners,' Dad had explained, waving The Book at us. 'And it's about who is top dog.'

Lexie rolled her eyes. 'Yes, Dad, I think he's getting the picture. He is just a *dog* you know …'

'Exactly!' said Dad, triumphant.

While I'm brushing my teeth I watch Zoom trying to round up Snow and Red. The guinea pigs hadn't lasted long back in the hutch before we let them free range again.

'They seem to have settled into an understanding,' Mum says, watching the action through the kitchen window. 'I think those pigs know Zoom's not going to catch them. He's had a hundred chances and he hasn't yet, so he obviously gets it. He knows he's not allowed.'

'He does get close, though,' I say, watching him chase Red into the ferns.

'It's all show,' says Mum. 'He *knows*.'

I hope so.

I hear a noise out the front, and stand on my tippy-toes to see over the gate. It's a guy on a scooter putting something in our letterbox.

'Woowoowoowoowoowoo!' shouts Zoom, his nose pointed high in the air. He bolts over to the gate and pokes his nose through the little hole that lets you get at the latch from outside.

'WOOF! WOOF WOOF WOOF!'

'Zoom! Shush,' I say. 'It's just the newspaper guy, it's okay!'

'WOOF! WOOF WOOF WOOF!'

'ZOOM!' I hear Dad shout from inside. 'Put a sock in it!'

'I don't really think he can understand that instruction,' Mum says.

The scooter guy accelerates off to Mrs Lucciano's place. Still on my tippy-toes I watch him as he pokes a newspaper into her letterbox, which is surrounded by pretty red and pink flowers.

'WOOF! WOOF! WOOF!' Zoom says as he goes, following up with a long growl.

'ZOOM!' Dad flings open the screen door. 'Stop it,' he says in a dark, low voice. 'That's *enough*.'

'Woof,' Zoom says half-heartedly through the hand-hole.

'No barking!' Dad barks, staring at him for a moment and then stomping back inside. 'He's getting worse.' Dad looks around for someone to say something, but no one does.

'He can't bark at just anyone who dares to walk up our street,' he says. 'It's intimidating.'

It's pretty hard to upset Dad, so I reckon he must be a bit stressed about work or something.

I go over to Zoom and stroke his head. He looks at me with his brown eyes and does one last general growl before dropping down onto the brick paving.

'Good boy,' I say, 'that's it. Calm kelpie.'

Maybe he thinks it's his job, to tell us someone is nearby? I smile at him.

Can dogs understand what a smile means, I wonder?

'Time for me to get going,' I say, scratching his thick neck fur. 'I'll see you this arvo, Zoom.'

He looks at me and I wish I could tell what he is thinking. Poor thing. He's been in trouble twice already today and it's still only morning!

Zoom gets into trouble with the authorities – the first time

I pull my bike through the gate after school and slam it shut behind me. That'll slow down Lexie a bit. I challenged her to a race home and want her to find me relaxing at the counter with a snack and a drink like I've been here for *ages* when she comes in.

Zoom lunges at Red, chasing him into the fountains of ferns. 'Zoom,' I say. 'Leave them alone.'

He comes over for a pat. Zoom's looking flash in his smart new collar, which Dad bought on the weekend because the one he's had since he was a little puppy got too snug. 'Be nice,' I say, looking quickly into the garden bed for Red's signature dreadlocks.

'Hello love,' says Mum. 'How was your day?'

I grab the water jug and scoop a handful of ice

cubes into my favourite glass. 'Good thanks, we made rockets with Mr Portelli and they went so high! He filmed it and is going to show us on the smartboard tomorrow.'

Mum smiles. 'Mr Portelli makes everything fun, by the sounds of it.'

I gulp the water and it's so cold going down that it almost hurts.

'Where's your sister?'

'Not far behind. What did you do today, Mum?'

'Well, it's been a busy day … Zoom decided to take himself on a, let's say, *self-guided walk*.'

I put my glass down. 'Oh, no.'

'Oh yes,' her eyes widen. 'And the ranger had to bring him back.'

'Is Zoom in trouble?'

'Well, thankfully, Zoom's registered and fully vaccinated and everything, so, no. And the ranger said she could tell he's still a puppy and was really good about it. Just said we need to keep an eye on him.'

'But how did he get out?'

'I think I mustn't have shut the gate properly.'

'Ohh …' I give her a smile. 'It is a bit sticky. I always have to really slam it to make the latch drop down.'

Mum nods. 'I'm going to spray some WD-40 on it, so

that should help. Anyway, the ranger picked him up —
guess where?'

There's only one place I can think of. 'The oval?'

She nods. 'The. Oval. And guess what he was doing
down there?'

I think about that. 'I don't know, was he … sniffing
around the tree trunks?'

'No.'

I think again. Zoom breaks out into a bark. Lexie
pushes open the gate.

'Zoomy, it's only me,' she calls.

'Chasing the birds? No — I know — eating some
old chips or something near the bins.'

Mum sighs. 'Hello Lex. No, Eli, nothing normal like
that.'

'How'd *you* get home so fast?' Lexie eyeballs me.

'Jetpack.' I lean back and take a long drink of water,
ice cubes chinking perfectly.

She rolls her eyes and drops her schoolbag to the
floor. 'Hi Mum.'

'So,' I say, 'If he wasn't sniffing tree trunks, chasing
birds or eating someone else's dropped chips, what was
he doing?'

'What are you talking about?' says Lexie.

'Zoom escaped today.'

'Escaped?'

'Yep.'

'Wow,' she says. 'Is he okay?'

'He wanted to visit the oval, apparently,' says Mum.

'What for?'

'He must have heard the lawnmowers.'

I laugh. 'No way. He did not.'

'Yes way, he did. There were two down there and he did his usual lawnmower dance around them, according to the ranger.'

I look at Zoom. He's lying on his bed, head on his front paws. 'Those ears of yours are really supersonic, Zoom!'

'And the council guys called the ranger and ... well, you know the rest.'

'Dad won't be very happy when you tell him about this,' says Lexie.

Mum takes a breath. 'No, he won't. And there's something else.'

'What?'

'This.' Mum walks towards a cardboard box on the table. She brings it over to us and holds it out so we can see inside.

'Oh no,' I groan.

There are about twenty socks in there. A few of

mine, including one of my footy socks and a thick red one which, with the other half, I wear when it's really cold.

'They're my new pair!' Lexie's hand pokes into the box and retrieves a perfect, brand new white sock. 'Well, one of them.'

'And Dad's Explorers,' Mum says. 'About four different halves. And my gardening socks!'

I lean away as she holds one up. Phew!

'I know, sorry,' she says. 'They were about to go in the wash. Until our Sock Thief here went on a rampage. I found all of these in what I can only describe as a sock *nest* on his bed this afternoon.'

We all look at Zoom.

'Do you think he knows he's done something wrong?' I ask.

'Why would he do that with the socks?' asks Lexie.

'You tell me, love. To build a sock empire?'

'It's his hobby,' I say, but I'm not so sure anymore.

'It's driving me to distraction,' grumbles Mum.

You can't go on a road trip without lollies

One morning when I wake up, Mum's busy in the kitchen and Dad is bringing in the esky from the shed.

'What's happening?' I blink, trying to figure out what day it is.

'Well, seeing it's such a beautiful day, we thought it would be nice to go on a picnic,' Mum says, popping a packet of my favourite biscuits into our camping crate.

'We'll drive up through the hills and then see where our noses lead us.'

I stretch and nod. 'Cool!'

I wash my face, pull on my comfiest shorts and the Dockers T-shirt I got for Christmas and get myself a bowl of cereal. From my spot at the kitchen bench I can see all the supplies Mum's packing for the day, as well as the extra things that Dad sneaks in, like the bag of liquorice allsorts that he tucks on top.

'You're hopeless,' Mum chuckles.

'Call me whatever you want; you can't go on a road trip without lollies for the drive.'

I grin. 'Onya, Dad!'

Zoom comes asking for a pat. Or maybe he's just hoping for some food? I smooth my hand over his head and ears. 'Good morning, fella. We're going on an adventure today.'

I turn to Mum. 'Are we taking Zoom?'

'Definitely! We just need to remember to bring some poo bags.'

Dad adds compostable bags to our supplies.

'He'll love it where we're going. Loads of new smells to sniff.'

'And different things to wee on,' says Lexie, coming out of her room. 'When are we leaving?'

We drive through the hills and stop to see the view of the city from the top. Lexie reads most of the way but I like looking out the window. In the luggage area behind us, Zoom pads from one side of the car to the other and makes little whining noises.

'Why can't he relax?' says Mum.

'He's excited,' says Dad. 'He'll settle down.'

I reach back and give him a pat. 'It's okay, Zoom,' I say. 'You can lie down if you want.'

But he doesn't. He's on high alert, looking out the window. Now I think about it, he never lies down in the car anymore. Not since he was a tiny puppy.

'Ooh, is that a drive-through coffee place?' says Mum. 'Let's just pop in there quickly.'

I roll my eyes. 'Mum, you have a coffee problem.'

'I know. Would you kids like a smoothie?'

Lexie's head lifts. 'Yes please!' she says.

'Do they have banana?' I ask.

Once she's taken our order, the woman serving us asks, 'Would your dog like a treat?'

Mum grins, and looks at Zoom. 'He would love that. Thank you!'

Coffees, smoothies and doggie-bone-shaped biscuit all handed out (and munched down in a nano-second), we get back on the road.

'We're heading east,' Dad says, 'where the bush meets farming country. Heaps of space to roam. I've always wanted to explore this neck of the woods.'

We drive for another hour or so. The cars get fewer and the trees get bigger. We pass huge road trains going towards the city.

Finally, we pull off the highway onto a smaller side road. We drive along for a while and then turn onto a gravel track. Dad drives slowly, bushes brushing the side of the car. The track opens out into a big area with a picnic table under trees.

'This looks perfect,' says Mum.

We put Zoom on his lead and hop out of the car. Dad groans and rubs his back.

My feet crunch as I walk around following Zoom. The ground is rocky and the trees spread their branches like long arms.

Zoom's ears twitch and move.

'Stay close,' Dad says.

'I'm just having a wee!' calls Lexie, walking away towards a clump of bushes. 'Nobody look!'

Zoom puts his nose on the gravel and has a big long sniff.

'What is it, Zoom, what can you smell?'

He moves away in a zig-zag, pulling on the lead, nose to the ground, stopping occasionally to focus on interesting smell-spots.

'It's a bit like metal-detecting, isn't it, mate?' says Dad. 'Except you don't find precious metals, you find precious …'

'Pongs?' I try.

'I think that's a fair guess.' Dad grins. 'Precious pongs,' he repeats, then laughs out loud.

Man can't get enough pickles

Mum pulls out the thermos and some mugs.

'You've just *had* a coffee!' Lexie says.

'That was ages ago,' Mum winks. 'And you should know by now that one coffee is never enough.'

'There's a cool trail over here going into the bush,' I call. 'Can we explore?'

'Just hang five,' Dad says, 'and we'll all go together.' He rustles around in the crate. 'Biscuit?'

'Oh, if you insist,' Mum says.

I tromp over and take two, hoping no one will notice. 'Then can we go?'

'Right, love, drink your coffee,' Dad says. 'These kids want action!'

Zoom and I lead the way down the path. It's quite narrow so we have to walk single-file. There are huge boulders in the bush and all sorts of different plants and trees, which Mum keeps trying to identify.

'Oh, look, is that an orchid?'

'Hmm, I don't know,' says Dad, stopping to investigate. 'It could be a spider orchid, I think they grow around here.'

'Seriously, this does not need to be like an episode of *Gardening Australia*,' huffs Lexie. 'Can we just keep walking?'

I turn to see Mum making a face and Dad trying not to laugh.

There's a rustle ahead of us and Zoom yanks on the lead so hard I nearly let go. He shoves his head into a bush, sniffs excitedly, and burrows in a little further before backing out. A moment later, when we crest a hill, he pauses, looking back at Mum and Dad and Lexie. He's waiting for them. As soon as he sees them he trots off again, tugging me along.

'He seems to quite like keeping an eye on us, doesn't he?' says Mum.

'He's smart,' says Dad.

'Even if he does chase lawnmowers,' says Mum.

'And barks at anyone who walks by,' grumbles Dad. 'Though I suppose he's just doing his job — telling us there's a stranger near our property.'

'He's protecting us,' Mum agrees.

'What about when he barks at Mrs Lucciano's cat though?' says Dad.

'That's a different sort of bark,' I say. 'More of a cat bark.'

'Seems like we need a bark-decoding device.'

Mum stops for a drink from her water bottle. 'Doesn't The Book have something to say about barking? Or about sock fixations? Any brilliant advice on those problems?'

'I'll have a look,' Dad mumbles.

'Hey, look!' I lower my voice and point. 'On that branch. That tree, there!'

Everybody stops in their tracks and follows my arm. 'There, see? It's a bird of prey. You can tell by the hooked beak.'

It cocks a regal eye at us.

'Would you look at that,' whispers Dad. 'Well spotted, Eli. That's a kite of some kind, I think.'

'What a beauty,' Mum says, smiling and watching.

The bird tilts its head to one side, then lightly lifts off the branch and hovers, using its powerful wings to stay in one spot.

'It's seen something,' Dad whispers.

It drops to the ground, fast and straight, and disappears from sight.

'I wonder what it saw?' says Lexie.

A moment later the bird flies back up into view. It's gripping something in its claws. 'Oh my goodness,' Mum whispers. 'It's got a mouse!'

'Nature in action.' Dad shakes his head in wonder. 'That's a fat little mouse, too.'

'Poor thing.' Lexie pouts.

Mum nods sympathetically. 'We can only hope it was quick.'

Zoom looks at us, as if to ask what we're doing. But he waits too, as patiently as he can, lifting a paw off the ground like he's about to take off in a one-hundred-dred-metre sprint.

When Dad finally says, 'Let's go,' we crunch along the track again and Zoom pulls ahead, as far as the lead will let him, the leader of our pack.

'Why don't we just use the table?' says Dad.

'Where's your sense of romance? And adventure?' Mum says. 'The table's the easy option. Let's go further afield.'

So we walk into the bush with all our food and find a flat area between tall trees where Lexie and I put the picnic blanket.

'I knew the rug would be useful,' Mum sings as she opens paper parcels of fresh ham and salami. 'It spends all year in the cupboard, getting musty, so it must be happy being out for once.'

'For goodness sake, it doesn't have feelings, love, it's just a *picnic blanket*.'

I look down. 'There's ants here.'

'Of course there are ants, Eli, we're in the bush.'

'They're crawling on our rug, though.'

'Just flick them off.'

I try, but every time I get one off, another five come on.

'Okay, here we go,' says Dad, bringing over some plastic plates and a giant Jenga pile of bread.

'And here are the fillings,' says Mum. She puts down the meats, a plate with slices of tomato, cucumber and cheese, a small bag of leaves and a bottle of mayo.

'Yum, I am so hungry,' I say, grabbing my tummy.

'Well, get it before the ants do,' Dad grins. Then he looks around, as if he's missing something. 'We didn't happen to bring the pickles, did we?'

Lexie groans. 'You will *not* die without pickles in your sandwich, Dad!'

'He actually will, though,' I laugh. 'Look at that face!'

Whistling is something I'm still working on

I slap my leg where I can feel something crawling. Dad flicks a couple of big ants off the blanket.

I reckon this is the best sandwich I've ever made. I didn't just have salami, which is my go-to favourite, but I put a slice of ham in too, and then layers of tomato, cheese and cucumber, finished with a big long squirt of mayo. And no yucky leaves.

While we're eating I get a funny feeling. I stop chewing and look around. 'Where's Zoom?'

The others sit up and look into the bush.

I stand up. 'Zoom!'

Mum calls him.

Dad calls him.

Lexie yells for him.

I force down my mouthful and try to whistle, but not much comes out. Whistling is something I'm still working on.

I listen for his paws on the dirt, for the sound of him galloping towards us — he never walks anywhere! But there's nothing apart from the dry shuffling of leaves in the trees around us.

'Zoom!' Dad booms. 'Wasn't he on the lead?'

'He was. I tied him up.' I scan the area and see a red looping snake-thing on the ground. It's a few metres away, among the leaves. I crunch over.

It's not a snake. I feel sick, pick it up.

'Oh no,' I turn to the others, Zoom's red lead in my hand.

'Where is he?' cries Lexie, looking at Mum, then Dad.

Mum clicks her tongue. 'He must have got off somehow. Naughty boy.'

Lexie looks at me. 'Did you tie him up properly, Eli?'

'Yesssss!' I turn my back to her.

'Now, now,' Mum cuts in. 'No, Lexie, that's not fair. There's no one to blame here. Eli knows how to manage Zoom's lead, he's done it dozens of times.'

'Well how did he get off?'

'He's a puppy, in an exciting environment, Lex,' Dad says. 'Naughty puppy business, that's all.'

'*Yeah*,' I say, flashing my eyes at her.

'Having said that, WHY can't he just sit still and lie around when we're doing something like this?' says Dad. 'Like a normal dog.'

'He may look fully grown but technically he's still a puppy,' Mum says.

Zoom's not a lying-around kind of dog, I want to say. *He doesn't sleep when there's smells to sniff and tracks to explore!* But I keep quiet. *Did* I tie him up properly?

Mum holds her hand up and listens. 'There are no ride-on mowers out here, are there?'

Dad groans. 'Right, let's go and have a scout around,' he says. 'Lexie, why don't you and I go back along the track and see if he's gone along there. And Eli, you go with Mum and have a really good look in the bush around here.'

I nod.

'But stay together!' says Dad. 'And take some water with you.'

Mum quickly packs away the food and I help her load the crate into the back of the car. 'We don't want the ants having a feast while we're gone,' she says.

We grab our water bottles. Mum has kept out the

packet of biscuits and slides them into a pocket on the side of her pants. 'I've always wondered what those pockets were for.'

I look at her. 'Biscuits, of course!'

She smiles and puts her arm around my shoulders. 'Exactly.' Then she takes a breath. 'It'll be all right, you'll see,' she says, giving me a squeeze.

I purse my lips and blow. Nothing. I lick my lips and adjust my tongue and try again. Any sound disappears with the wind. 'I wish I could *whistle*,' I say. 'Why is it so hard?'

'It took me years to learn how to whistle,' Mum says as we push between bushes and duck under low branches. 'Your Uncle Pete was a whistling champion, he could whistle with his fingers and everything,' she says. 'But all I could blow was air.'

'Shhhh.' Was that something? We stop and listen. 'What was it?'

'Not sure,' I say. 'Must have been nothing.'

We keep going and come to a fence. 'Oh, so this must be the start of a property,' Mum says. 'Private land. A farm, I guess.'

We walk along the fenceline for a while, calling, 'Zoom, Zoom!' but he doesn't come. He isn't anywhere here. If he'd heard us, he would have come. I know it.

Mum changes direction. We're angling back towards where we had our lunch. She stops and scratches her head, then pulls out the biscuits. 'This calls for sustenance,' she says. Her voice is cheerful but her face is worried. 'Where is he?'

I listen hard for paws on the ground, scrunching leaves, Zoom's pink-tongued panting.

'Let's head back to the car and see if Dad and Lexie have found him. He can't have got too far.'

Dad's sitting at the picnic table when we get back. 'Nothing,' he says, and looks at Mum.

My heart sinks.

'We went all the way back along the track, but he wasn't anywhere there.' Lexie's eyes are filling up. 'He must be really lost!'

A dog doesn't need roads

Dad spreads out a big map. His fingers trace a path to where we are now. 'Let's see where he could have gone, Eli.'

I look at the map with Dad. It's hard to understand, a weird puzzle with jagged green shapes and yellow wiggly lines cutting through them.

Dad's fingers take off in different directions. Every now and then he looks up and around, and mutters, 'Aaah, I see,' or 'So that's *that* road,' and 'Hmm, that looks steep.'

'What do you think, Dad?' Flies buzz around my face. I swish at them but they don't go away for long. One lands on the corner of my lips. 'Pfffft!' I blow it off in disgust.

He slides his hand back and forth across his forehead.

'Zoom!' Mum calls into the bush, then walks in another direction. 'Zoom!'

'To be honest, mate, he could have gone anywhere. This just helps us know where *we* are. And where the roads are. But of course, a dog doesn't need roads.'

Over the next hour we call and call and I try all the different ways to whistle. We take turns looking at the map, hoping it might help us find Zoom.

'I'm just hoping his cheeky face will pop out of the bush any minute now,' Mum says, passing around the biscuits. She takes the last one and scrunches up the packet.

Dad glances at his watch, but doesn't say anything.

'Let's go back to where we had our picnic,' I suggest, 'in case he's waiting there for us.'

'I'll come,' says Lexie.

'Stay together,' Mum says.

We make lots of noise as we walk, hoping Zoom will hear us but also I remember Mr Portelli telling us that snakes don't like noise-vibrations. They don't have ears so can't actually hear anything, but they can *feel* noise. I carry a big stick and deliberately stomp on all the dry leaves on the path.

Lexie points. 'That's where Mum put the picnic blanket.' Then she bends down and giggles. 'And that's one of my sandwich crusts. Covered in ants. Lucky them.'

'Zoom! Here boy!' I call.

'Zoomy Zoom, come, come, we're here,' Lexie yells.

We stand still, listening for any sounds of movement in the bush. But other than the screeches of black cockatoos, there's nothing.

'He's not here,' I say. My chest feels funny.

Lexie looks at me and gives another big call-out. We wait, not moving.

'What are we going to do?'

She chews her lip. 'I don't know. He's definitely not here. Let's go back to Mum and Dad.'

When we reach the picnic table area Dad and Mum look at us hopefully. 'He wasn't there,' Lexie says. 'He would have come if he was nearby — we called really loudly.'

'Right,' says Dad.

'Unless he's hurt,' says Mum quietly.

We turn to her.

She shakes her head. 'Oh, I don't know … I just wondered if he's maybe caught in a trap — for feral cats or foxes — or has his leg stuck in a fence or something.'

'Possible,' says Dad.

'But unlikely,' says Mum.

'Time's not working in our favour,' Dad tilts his head at the sky. 'There's not a lot of light left.'

'We can't leave him out all night!' Lexie says.

'We might not have any choice.'

Mum pulls out her phone. 'I think it's time we called the ranger.'

'But won't they take him to the pound if they find him?' I say. 'Remember Max's story about what happens to dogs at the pound, Dad?'

'The pound is actually a safe place for an animal to stay while the rangers look for the owners—'

'Us,' I say. '*We're* the owners. We *want* Zoom, unlike some of those other people. We want him a lot.'

'Exactly. So if the rangers find Zoom they'd call us and we'd go and collect him.'

'Not …'

'No, absolutely not,' Dad says. 'That only happens when the rangers have done everything they can to find the owner and, failing that, when they can't find a new home for the pooch. It's a last resort, Eli.'

My heart is beating hard. I take a breath.

Dad puts his arm around my shoulder while Mum does a quick search on her phone. I watch her thumb as she presses CALL.

Someone answers and Mum explains what has happened, which takes a while. Then she presses the speaker icon so we can all hear the person on the other end. It's a man's voice.

'There's not much we can do at this time of the day,' he says. 'We knock off at 6pm. Your pup will show up,' he says reassuringly. 'They usually do, after they've had a bit of mischief. We'll just have to wait and see where he ends up. Hopefully on one of the neighbouring farms, and not the highway.'

Mum's eyes flick to Dad.

Dad groans.

'We know most of the farmers around here. They'll give us a ring if they see him. Your dog … he's microchipped, you say?'

'Yes,' says Mum.

'And he's black, a kelpie cross?'

'Yes.'

I jab towards the phone. 'He has a little white flame on his chest.'

Mum smiles. 'That's our son, Eli. He and his sister

are worried, as I'm sure you can understand.'

'I certainly can understand that,' the ranger says. 'Look, how about I get on the two-way now and tell all my staff, just in case the rangers out on patrol are nearby and can do a quick look-see … What's the pooch's name again? Zed? Zorro?'

'Zoom!' says Lexie.

'Ahh, that's right — Zoom by name, zoom by nature, by the sounds of it. Am I right?'

'Yes, you are.' Mum shakes her head with a smile.

'Once I've put out the alert I'll leave a note on our job board so all staff members know we're looking for a black kelpie cross — with a white flame. Then everyone will be on the job.'

'Thank you so much for your help,' Mum says.

Dad leans towards the phone. 'Would you recommend we wait here, or …?'

'Look, there's not much point staying out, to be honest. He's been gone so long now it's unlikely he'll go back to where you started, given it's an unusual place for him. If it were somewhere he knew well and you took him often, I'd suggest you stay put — sometimes they find their way back. But this is different.'

I swallow.

The ranger goes on. 'I'd say head on home. We have

your number and if we find him, we'll call. We'll look after him. And if he needs medical care we'll get him to our local vet who looks after all our animals.'

If he needs medical care! Lexie and I stare at each other.

'Okay, right.' Dad clears his throat. 'Thanks so much for your help. We're … really sorry about this.'

'Don't worry, these things happen. I'm sure we'll get him back to you.'

Mum slides her phone into her pocket.

Alert: black kelpie, white flame

'We can't just leave Zoom out here!' I blurt. 'He'll be looking for us. If we drive home he won't be able to sniff his way back to us.'

Dad folds up the map. I can tell he's thinking.

'Eli—

'—and there are wedge-tailed eagles around! You've told us before how they sometimes take baby goats and lambs from farms. Maybe they'd take a pu—'

'No, Eli,' Mum says. 'That is *not* going to happen.'

'Zoom would bark the socks off any eagle trying to have a go at him,' Dad ruffles my hair. 'Though wedgies don't tend to wear socks, I'll give you that …'

'Dad!' Lexie protests.

'Sorry. But seriously, you know what Zoom's like — when he sees Mrs Lucciano's cat, for instance. He barks and he is LOUD! Lambs and baby goats, they can't make scary barking noises to defend themselves. No, I reckon Zoom would be able to hold his own in that situation.'

'My stomach hurts,' I say.

Mum pulls me into a big, warm, safe hug.

'Maybe we could sleep in the car tonight?' I suggest.

Mum and Dad look at each other. 'We're not sleeping in the car,' Dad says. 'My back isn't up for that sort of caper anymore.'

'There are a couple of hotels nearby,' Mum's voice brightens. 'We could go and have a look, maybe—'

'— have a pub dinner!' says Dad. 'Mmmm, now you're talking.'

'And then we wouldn't be too far away if the ranger calls us,' Lexie adds.

'*When*,' says Dad. 'When the ranger calls us.'

I nod, still in Mum's hug.

'And what I was *going* to say, before Dad got all excited about *food* and interrupted me,' says Mum, 'was that we could maybe even stay overnight at the hotel, if they have a room.'

'And *that* way we can resume the search at first light,' says Dad, nodding at Mum. 'Very smart, my love, very smart indeed. That's why they pay Mum the big bucks, kids.'

Mum laughs.

I squeeze her. She really is the best.

Dad goes for the steak sandwich, with extra pickles. Mum has chilli mussels, Lexie has the chicken schnitzel and I have my all-time fave — a burger and chips. It's huge, and juicy, and comes with bacon. There's also a salad on the side which makes Mum happy.

I don't think I'll be able to eat, but when the meal comes I realise how hungry I am. During dinner I keep my eye on Mum's phone in case it rings.

Dad scrunches up his paper napkin, leans back and sighs.

Lexie looks at Mum's phone, then at me.

'I think a little walk might be needed after that.' Dad pats his stomach.

'Do we still have the torch in the glovebox, Dad?' Lexie asks.

He nods. 'I think so. Why?'

Lexie bites the inside of her lip. 'I just thought if we're going for a walk, we could look at the bush around here, in case …'

'Do a bit of spotlighting for Zoom?' He nods. 'Good idea.'

Dad scrummages around in the glovebox while Mum holds her phone torch for him to see by.

'Ha!' He leans back out, holding a large black torch with a long barrel. 'Try this,' he says, passing it to me.

I press the button on the torch and a solid white beam cuts into the bush, lighting up gum trees like ghosts.

'Working!' I say.

'Look at that,' Dad says. 'Now *that's* a torch.'

'I'll use my phone torch,' says Mum. 'Let's go in pairs and we'll have enough light to see while we walk.'

There's a sudden rustle a few metres away, at the edge of the bush.

'What was that?' I swing my torch beam across the area.

'Sounded big,' says Lexie in a small voice.

'Everything sounds big at night when you're in the bush,' says Dad. 'Don't be spooked. It's probably just a blue-tongue lizard finding his bed for the evening.'

I step towards the bush, the hotel behind me. 'Zoom,' I call, then louder: 'Zoom!'

'We'll go this way then,' Mum says, walking

with Lexie away from us. 'To maximise our success potential.'

'Right,' says Dad. 'Yell out if you have any luck.'

'Or if you see any snakes,' I say.

'Shhh,' says Dad. 'Don't even suggest it.' He whistles, clear and sharp into the night. 'Zoom!'

My feet crunch on the ground. The torch is super powerful, lighting the way ahead and beyond.

I stop still. 'What's that? That sound?'

Around us is a low rising sound like a moped in the distance, except this isn't in the distance, it's right here. And I definitely can't see a moped.

Dad grins. 'That's a motorbike frog.'

I listen again. The sound builds, like an engine speeding up.

'That's amazing!'

'They're perfectly named, aren't they?'

'Wow.' I grin, and keep walking. 'Zoom!' I call, flashing the big torch deeper into the bush.

We hear Mum's voice calling Zoom, too. 'Well if he's out here anywhere he'll hear us,' says Dad. 'Where on earth has he taken himself off to? *Zoom!*'

'He probably just got curious in the nose, Dad. He's still a puppy.'

'True.'

'Do you think he's scared?' I ask, 'out here, on his own?'

'Well, I don't know …' Dad's feet crunch in time with mine. 'I don't think he'd be scared of the bush, but he might be scared to not be in his usual bed, at home with us, I suppose.'

'And far away from any socks.'

Dad laughs. 'He'll be suffering sock deprivation, that's for sure.'

I scan a tree not far from us. The light catches something red and glinting.

'Hey, what's that?' Dad's voice drops to a whisper.

I go backwards with the torch. Red. Glinting.

'That!' hisses Dad.

'Eyes!' I say.

I adjust the torch to focus the beam more sharply on the red eyes.

'A possum?' I ask.

Dad squints into the dark. 'I don't think so …' He reaches out for the torch and holds it steady. 'Have another look, Eli. You know what this guy is.'

I look at Dad and drop my jaw. 'A cat!'

'A monster.'

'There aren't any houses around here,' I say, 'so it can't be someone's pet.'

'It's a feral. Look how big it is, and how it's just staring at us. Not scared at all. Monsters of the Australian bush, they are,' Dad says.

I take back the torch while Dad vents.

'They kill millions of native animals every year, Eli, did you know that? Millions!' Dad's glaring at it.

'Maybe Zoom will get him,' I say. 'He *hates* cats.'

'Zoom!' I call. But there's no doggy movement in the bush, or anything Zoom-like.

I sweep the torch across the whole area. 'Where *is* he, Dad?'

Dad takes in a long breath and looks around. 'I reckon he's more likely to be closer to where we were today.'

Suddenly there's a piercing scream. I recognise the sound immediately and by the look of Dad's face, so does he.

'Lexie!' I yell.

The original jump scare

Even in the torchlight I can see Dad's face lose colour.

He spins around to face the direction of her voice. 'Lexie!' he shouts. 'Lexie, we're coming! Are you okay?' He grabs my hand and holds me still while we wait for a response.

But there's nothing. Total silence.

My heart has relocated to the soft part of my throat, it's thudding like crazy.

'Where are you?' Dad calls really loudly. 'Lexie!'

He looks at me, eyes fearful.

'LEXIE!' I yell.

'Lexie,' Dad calls from some place deep in his belly. 'Kate! KATE!'

No answer.

'KATE, LEXIE!'

We crunch and trip and run in the direction of Lexie's scream.

'We're coming!' I yell.

The torchlight judders over the bush as we run, leaping over rocks on the path and ducking under branches.

Dad stops suddenly and I nearly faceplant his back. 'Call out so we can come to you,' he says into the dark.

Finally, we hear Mum. 'Over here!' She sounds close.

We move towards her voice, more slowly now.

Suddenly, to my left, I see a big shape on the ground. 'Dad, torch, here!'

As the light swings over we see Mum, with dirt, leaves and twigs all over her. She's on the ground, on all fours, looking over a ledge. She's shining her phone torch into the space.

'Kate!' Dad goes straight to her and drops down. 'What happened? Are you okay?'

'Yes,' she croaks, 'but Lexie ... She thought she heard a dog yelping and she pelted towards it.' Mum sobs. 'She said it sounded like Zoom. And then, she just disappeared, over that ledge. I tried to get her, but just couldn't see my way and—'

Dad points the torch over the ledge.

'Lexie!' he bellows. 'Lexie!'

There's no reply.

I quickly kneel next to Mum and put my arm around her back. 'Mum? Are you okay?'

Her face is strained but she says, 'I'm fine Eli. Just a bit scratched and sore. But Lexie—' she cranes over the rocky edge. 'She's down there somewhere.' Mum's shining her phone torch but the light isn't getting beyond a couple of metres.

I scamper up. 'I'm going down.'

'No, no, Eli—'

'Dad.' I take the torch from his hands. I have to prise it from his fingers.

I shine the torch around the area to see what I can see. The beam pierces through the dark, lighting up rocks and bushes. The motorbike frogs have gone quiet.

Lexie's down there, and maybe Zoom too. There's no way I'm not going.

It's steep, but doesn't look too hard to climb down. There's a lot of loose rocks and dirt, a few bushes and small trees.

Behind me, Mum groans and says, 'I've done my ankle. It's the size of a football.'

I'm already a few rocks down, and grab any plants within reach to stay steady. I shine the torch around. 'What's tha—?' I swing the light back to something that doesn't belong in the picture. 'Lexie!' I yell. 'There she is. *There she is!* I can see her!'

'Oh, thank all the gods,' Dad shouts.

'Lex! LEX! We can see you,' I yell. 'I'll come and get you.' There's no reply.

'He always was a mountain goat,' I hear Mum say.

Dad yells, 'Be careful, Eli, it's dangerous. We can call triple 0 if need be.'

I squat down where it gets tricky and test for wobbly rocks. Most are solid, but every now and then there's a dodgy one. My feet seem to get into a rhythm and go easily from rock to dirt, with my free hand reaching for clumps of bushes as I step and sometimes slide down.

'Lexie!' I call every few steps, but she doesn't respond.

I keep going and with every step the ground flattens a little and I realise I'm getting closer to the bottom of whatever this is. I can hear my breath in my ears.

'Lex,' I call again, my foot scraping awkwardly off a rock. Youch. I look down at my feet. *Take it easy*, I tell myself. *Slow down. Slow down.*

There's a big fallen tree ahead of me and I stop and sweep my torch along the fat trunk, and that's when I see her, sitting on the ground leaning against the trunk. She has a bloody gash in her head and is blinking like she's just woken up. She's holding her arm.

'Lexie,' I say, running to her. 'Are you okay?'

She looks at me. I can see she's been crying. 'Eli …'

'You've got a cut on your head, Lex.' It's just above her ear and looks yuck.

She tries to reach up to touch it but doesn't get far. 'Owww.' Her hand goes straight back where it was, tenderly supporting her other arm.

'My arm hurts. I— I fell down … and then rolled and — owwwwwww.' She moans and squeezes her eyes shut. 'I thought I heard Zoom, but it wasn't him. I'm so stupid.'

I give her a smile. 'It's okay. Mum and Dad are at the top. Do you think you can make it back up? I can help you.'

She swipes her nose with her shoulder.

'I don't know.'

'Eli!' We hear Dad's voice. 'How're you going?'

I stand and shout towards him, 'I've found her, Dad, she's okay. She's … got a cut on her head and a sore arm.'

As I say that I shine the torch on Lex's arm and see that it's a strange shape, a bit like a banana … I quickly flick the torch away as seeing it makes me feel queasy.

I nod at Lexie and look up the rocky slope. 'We can do this, can't we, sis?'

Lexie steps gingerly towards it. She looks up, then

nods. 'Yep. I'm going to need your help though, Eli.'

I peer into the darkness. 'I'll go first, so you can see the way. Just tell me if you need to stop or if you need a hand.'

We take it slow, and a few times I have to help Lex balance, because with that banana arm she's all wonky. Once I grab her T-shirt so she doesn't fall.

Somehow it works, partly because I know the way this time, and partly because we're heading towards safety.

'Not far now,' I say, as Lex's face crumples in pain. 'We're almost there.'

Dad's shining the weakening glow of Mum's phone towards us. 'Just take one step at a time,' he says, his voice husky. 'You are a bloody champion, Eli.'

And while Lex catches her breath a couple of steps away from the top, I hear the slow, even croak of a motorbike frog starting up, as though it's coming with us for the ride.

Lots of limping and groaning

Dad and I help Mum and Lexie back to the hotel. There's a fair bit of limping and groaning.

'My arm's a strange shape,' Lexie says, looking at it.

'Straight into the car, everyone,' Dad says. 'We're going to the hospital.'

While Dad drives, Mum and Lexie jumble out the whole story.

'I heard this sound and was sure it was Zoom.'

'I tripped at the ledge,' says Mum, 'And that's when I did this ankle. I grabbed a bush to stop myself from sliding in further, but Lexie—'

'I just went right down, rolling and bumping like nothing else. I think I screamed, it was so scary.'

'You did!' I say. 'It was spooky. That's what made us come looking.'

'I was calling and calling you, Lex,' Mum says, 'But you might have got knocked out along the way because it got very very quiet after that.'

'I'm not sure, I can't remember the whole thing. But,' Lexie rolls her eyes, 'once I was down there, I realised it wasn't Zoom at all, it was just the weird sound of these two trees rubbing against one another. Seriously.'

'I think that must be an old quarry site or something, and we just didn't know it was there,' Dad says. 'We would *never* have walked out there at night had we known.'

'No, we wouldn't,' groans Mum. 'Not on a cold day in hell.'

'The hospital's just around this corner,' says Dad. 'It's a small local hospital so I reckon we'll get seen pretty quickly.'

'Grateful for small blessings,' Mum says.

'Grateful for Eli, saving his sister!' Dad says.

'Yeah!' says Lexie, trying to do a high-five but not getting far at all. 'Argh, it hurts …'

'Oh love,' Mum says, twisting in her seat. 'You poor thing. Thank goodness your brother got you out of there, otherwise it could have been far worse.' Mum squeezes my leg. 'You're our hero, Eli.'

I grin, and look out the window. The bush is big and black beyond the road. 'But what about Zoom?' I say, feeling a big weird hole in my tummy. 'I wish he had been down there, too. Where *is* he?'

Zoom, still lost

Mum's phone is ringing. I roll over, trying to escape the light shining on my face.

Then I remember: Zoom. Still lost.

And the phone's ringing.

'Mum,' I whisper as loudly as I can. 'Mum!'

She snaps upright like a cartoon character.

'Your phone.'

She grabs it from the bedside table and stabs at it wildly about three times before she picks up the call.

'Hello?' A man's voice.

'Hello, this is Kate.'

'Ah, Kate, hi, it's the ranger from Hills Council Animal Pound here, with a bit of an update for you.'

'Yes!' Mum says, shaking Dad awake. 'Thank you for calling … Have you found Zoom?'

'Well, no, I'm sorry to say that we haven't. I wanted to see if you'd had any luck before I head out to do a patrol.'

'Oh …' Mum breathes out. 'No, we haven't had any luck either. We stayed at the Frog Hollow Hotel last night though … had a bit of an adventure spotlighting, but that's another story … and we thought we'd head out to look for him shortly.'

Dad's awake now. 'We thought we'd go back to where we took him yesterday,' he says into the phone.

'That sounds sensible. I'll head to a couple of properties nearby and ask around. Sometimes they turn up overnight and the farmers don't realise for a few hours that they have another dog in the mix.' The ranger chuckles. 'Let me know if you have any luck and, of course, I'll do the same.'

Mum hangs up. Lexie's awake now and she's looking at her cast.

'Can you believe what happened last night?' she says.

Dad shakes his head. 'Actually, no, I can't. I'm pretty cross with myself for letting us get into that situation. It was a stupid thing to do.'

Mum gives him a hug. 'All we have to do is find Zoom, and then everything will be all right.'

Dad rubs his head. 'Ha, is that all?! If only it were that easy …'

'Well, let's get out there,' says Mum. 'Let's get dressed and we'll see if we can get some toasted sandwiches from somewhere on the way.'

'And coffee,' Dad says.

'And smoothies?' Lexie asks.

'And smoothies,' Mum agrees. 'It could be a long day, so we'll need all the sustenance we can get.'

We all look at each other.

'We have to find him — today,' I say.

Mum and Dad nod.

A man called Grub

Finally, brushing toasted-ham-and-cheese-sandwich crumbs from our faces and with a last slurp of the smoothie cups, Dad turns the car onto the gravel track where all this began yesterday.

We trundle down until we see the familiar picnic area under gum trees. I feel better somehow just for being here. Closer to Zoom.

We get out and stretch.

'Zoom!' I call, pretty well straight away.

'Zoomy Zoom,' Lexie calls, and follows it up with a good whistle.

I wet my lips, purse them, and blow. Nothing, just air. And, in the distance, the sound of sheep.

'So *this* time,' Dad says, 'We stay together.'

We're trying to decide which direction to walk

in when I hear a noise. Quite a big noise, actually. Movement in the bush.

Mum and Dad stop talking. Lexie spins around.

Suddenly, there's a big crash and the noise of animals. My mouth drops open.

A group of bleating, leaping sheep bursts into the clearing, making crazy mayhem. The ones at the back kick their rear legs, and some even leap onto the backs of others.

They move around like a big woolly jumble, desperately pressing against one another to stay together.

We all take a few steps back because they're coming this way.

'Woah!' says Mum, pushing up so she's perched on the bonnet of the car. I step up onto the picnic bench and stand on that, watching the shifting cloud of sheep move in. Lexie quickly joins me.

And then we see something coming up behind them, a familiar black shape.

Zoom!

He's running low to the ground around the group, weaving back and forth behind them.

'Zoom!' I yell.

'Zoom!' Mum cries. 'What —'

'Zoom!' Lexie's face breaks into a huge smile.

'Zoom,' Dad booms, his eyes big as he takes in the sheep. 'What … Oh no … What have you done here?'

But Zoom's busy with the sheep, shifting around them, creeping low to the ground, light-footed.

None of us moves. The sheep baa and huddle and jump over one another. There must be about twenty of them.

'Where on earth did you find them?' Dad says.

'It must have been — the fence, remember, Eli? We saw a fence on our walk yesterday,' Mum says, her words racing. 'They must have got onto the wrong side of the property, somehow.'

'Or Zoom jumped the fence to get amongst them,' Dad said, half-cross.

'Well, but then they must have jumped the fence too, to be on this side …'

'They couldn't have,' I say, trying to get Zoom's attention by slapping my knees. 'I saw the fence — there's no way these sheep could have jumped over that.'

'Zoom, here boy,' I call.

He completely ignores me, and moves around the sheep low like a fox, keeping them together.

We stare at the animals. They look at Zoom.

'Well … I — I don't know what we should do in this situation, to be honest,' Dad says, swallowing. '*Again.*'

Zoom curves around the outside of the bustling sheep one last time before quietly lying down at one side, looking very pleased with himself.

Then he looks at us.

'Me neither,' says Mum, taking a seat at one of the picnic tables. 'But look at him go.'

Then we hear another weird noise.

I turn to look down the gravel road. It sounds like an engine, and it's rumbling and grumbling towards us.

Dad swings around too, trying to pick the direction it's coming from. The sheep jitter and press up against one another in fear.

And then, into this patch of bush on this Super Weird Sunday thunders a man on an off-road motorbike. He sees us and pulls over.

'Is this the ranger?' Mum asks, confused.

'G'day,' the man says, grinning. Then he turns to the sheep and says, 'There you are!'

Dad says, 'They're yours? The sheep?'

'Sure are,' says the man. 'This is what I get for not fixing my fences!'

He walks over to Dad and offers his hand. 'Grub's the name.'

Dad shakes it and laughs, 'There'll be a story behind that, I bet.'

Grub nods, grinning. 'Yup.'

'So you're not the ranger?' Mum says. 'From Hills Council?'

Grub laughs. 'Me? Nah, I'm a farmer, got the property just over the way there. Is this your dog?' he reaches out his hand.

Zoom pads over to him, sniffs his hand, then licks it.

'G'day, boy,' Grub says quietly.

'Zoom!' Lexie says huffily. 'What about us?'

'Yes, it is, sorry,' says Dad. 'This is Zoom, and … well, it seems he's forgotten he's a city dog.'

'We're really sorry if he's caused you trouble,' says Mum.

'Trouble? Not at all, he's saved me! He's a good work dog, is what he is,' Grub says, leaning down for a proper pat.

None of us can believe what we're seeing. My head won't stop shaking like one of those bobble-head figurines people have in their cars.

'Zoom,' I eventually call, and crouch down. This time he trots over, and his fur feels so soft and good between my fingers. It's the best feeling ever. I bury my head against his neck and tell him I love him.

'He's a good worker, that dog, aren't ya, mate?' Grub says to him, to all of us. 'You're kelpie through and through, you are.'

Zoom's tail sweeps wide like the biggest smile.

'He's saved me a heap of bother. These girls would've gone much further without him,' Grub says. 'We had a problem with the perimeter fence yesterday and had to remove a small section, and I thought — well, I was wrong, I know that now, but I *thought* — we could get away with leaving that bit open for a night.' He shakes his head. 'Never thought the girls would press up into the paddock so far, and then cross through.'

I look at Lexie. She has a silvery mark down one cheek, and a huge smile on her face.

'Shows what fifteen years of farming has taught me,' he laughs. 'Never trust a flock of sheep given half a chance!'

'But how did Zoom know what to do with them?' asks Mum. 'He's never worked on a farm before.'

'His mum was a working dog, though,' Dad says.

'It's just instinct with these breeds,' says Grub, 'your border collies and kelpies. It's just in their genes. It's part of who they are.'

'He's been practising with the ride-on mowers at the oval!' I say.

Mum's jaw drops and she looks at me.

'Ha, likes to chase them, does he?' says Grub.

'Yes!'

'Maybe he's rounding 'em up.' Grub grins.

'I'd better get these girls back into the paddock,' he says, then nods at Zoom. 'You might want to hold your sheepdog so he doesn't come back to the farm with us.'

'I've got him!' I say, sliding my hand under his collar. I never want to let go of him again.

Grub starts his motorbike, and the sheep scatter like woolly marbles at the sudden noise. Zoom is alert, watching the action, ears turning this way and that.

The farmer crawls slowly behind the animals on his bike, keeping them together. He whistles and calls *Yah!* loud and strong.

We stand back until they're gone. I watch until I can't hear the motorbike anymore. Until all I can see is a cloud of dust, hanging in the air.

The world's best dog

'Zoom,' Dad says, ruffling the thick coat around his neck. 'We should be cross with you, but we're just so glad to have you back. You're a proper sheepdog, mate! Farmer Grub said so!'

'*Grub*,' says Lexie. 'That's so funny.'

'I can't believe it,' says Mum. 'How did Zoom find those sheep?'

'Maybe he smelled them on the wind?' says Dad rubbing Zoom's furry nose. 'This schnoz isn't for nothing, is it? All that sniffing training you've been doing down at the park …'

'And herding training,' says Mum.

'Clip this on him, Eli,' Dad says, passing me the lead. 'We don't want him going on any other adventures just now.'

I give Zoom the biggest hug ever as click the lead on. He looks so proud!

Lexie comes over with some leftover bread from our picnic yesterday. She tears it into pieces and Zoom gobbles it down.

'He must need some water, after all that running,' says Mum. She opens her bottle and looks around for something to pour it into.

'Coffee mug?' Dad says.

'Bit too small for his nose …'

We look around.

'Picnic plate?' suggests Lexie.

'Hmmm … too shallow,' says Mum.

'Here,' I say, cupping my hands together. 'Pour some in here, Mum.'

She does and I offer him my water bowl. He pokes his nose in, then laps til my hands are dry.

Mum refills the Eli-bowl and again, Zoom's pink tongue scoops up every drop and licks my hands with a velvety finish.

'He *is* thirsty,' says Dad.

Then Zoom burps. Loudly.

'Zoom!' Lexie laughs. 'That's rude!'

'Yes, paw over your mouth, please,' says Mum.

He lies down on the ground, blinking into the afternoon sun under the long-armed trees.

On the way home, for the first time since he was a tiny puppy, Zoom lies down in the back. I'm used to having his head next to ours, poking over the top of the seats. It makes it easy to reach him for pats. I think back to when we brought him home from Rob's farm, and how small he was, fitting into the laundry basket.

I turn to check on him. I have to do a double-take.

He's asleep.

'Mum, look! Lexie!'

Mum pushes up out of her seat to see him. Her mouth opens, and she looks at us. 'Well, there you go. Wonders will never cease!'

I watch him. His whiskers are twitching.

'He's dreaming!' I whisper.

'Dreaming of rounding up sheep,' Dad says, smiling.

'And his next adventure,' I murmur, stroking his head.

Then Lexie remembers: 'Dad! The liquorice allsorts!'

'*Yes!!*'

Mum flips open the glovebox. 'Two each!' she says, passing the packet around.

The rainbow stripes beam out at us. Lexie takes hers, then elbows me and opens her hand just enough so I can see three allsorts nestled in her palm. She grins at me. I quickly sneak three cubes without Mum noticing.

We smile out our windows so we don't give ourselves away.

Zoom's head pokes up behind us.

'Cheeky devil,' says Dad, chewing happily. 'But these are definitely not doggie treats.'

That night we order takeaway kebabs from the Turkish deli up the road for dinner. 'It's too late to cook now,' Dad says, unloading the esky into the fridge. 'Plus, I think we'd all agree, it's been a very big weekend!'

I feed Zoom and sit on the deck watching him crunch his dinner. He eats the chunks of meat first and then the biscuits. When the bowl is empty he licks it, just to make sure, and sniffs around on the lawn for any biscuits that fell out when he was eating. Sometimes the guinea pigs get the ones Zoom misses. Then he has another huge drink of water. When he's finished I take his water bowl to the outside tap and refill it, so it's ready for him when he needs another drink.

Zoom lies down on the cool grass and keeps an eye on Snow and Red.

Dad and Lexie come back from the Turkish shop and we sit down at the table in our spots.

'Who asked for tzatziki?' Mum asks, holding out a kebab. 'And here's yours with beetroot, Lex.'

We eat in silence for a couple of minutes. 'These have got to be the best kebabs in the whole world,' I say, closing my eyes as I chew.

Dad looks at Zoom. He's dozing on his bed. 'Well, Zoom,' he says. 'You really showed us who you are today.'

'"Kelpie, through and through." Isn't that what the farmer said?'

Zoom lifts his ears and turns to stare at us.

'You know we're talking about you,' I say, grinning.

'I think he really enjoyed being out in the bush,' says Mum. 'Plus, he got to do what he's best at.'

I feel sad then. 'Do you think … Is it *mean* that we

have him here in the city? Where there are no sheep?'

'Well,' says Mum. 'I think he has a good life here. He's surrounded by love, and we keep him active. But I know what you mean.'

'Maybe he misses being on the farm where he was born,' says Lexie.

I chew my lip. 'And being able to work.'

'Living his best kelpie life,' says Dad.

We look over at Zoom. He wags his tail and sits up neatly, like he does when he's hoping for a treat.

'But you *do* do kelpie things here in the city, don't you, Zoom?' I say.

The others wait for me to explain.

'Well, he has jobs here — and hobbies. Just … some of them we don't like much, like the lawnmower chasing.'

Lexie pipes up then. 'And telling us when the postie's here, or when someone is at the door, right Eli?'

I nod at her. 'Yeah. And getting the ball, *every single time* we throw it, even when he's tired.'

Mum nods slowly and says, 'And keeping the guinea pigs in the guinea-pig part of the garden.' She keeps nodding. 'I see what you're getting at.'

Dad says, 'And by "hobbies", you mean …'

'You know. Sock collecting.'

Mum and Dad nod.

We all sit back in our chairs.

'Could we … maybe take Zoom to a farm sometimes?' I say. 'Now that we know he's a champion working dog.'

'I've been wondering the same thing,' says Dad. 'So he can keep up his working dog skills.'

'Just for short visits,' I say. 'Not to stay.'

'Oh, I think he would love that,' says Mum.

'Maybe the farmer we got him from would let us take him back there sometimes?'

Dad looks at Mum, then back at me. 'You know what? I reckon he might.'

'We can only ask him,' Mum says.

Zooms looks at me. I feel really good.

'Look at him,' Lexie croons. 'Is he *smiling*?'

'That's certainly the face of a happy pooch,' Mum says. 'We're lucky to have such a great dog.'

'So lucky Max came over that evening,' I say. 'What would we do without you, Zoom?'

'Even if he does bark a bit more than he needs to,' says Dad.

Mum throws Dad a big smile. 'Weren't you going to check what The Book says about that?'

'*Yeah Dad*,' Lexie and I say together.

That night, I'm in bed reading when I hear Zoom just outside my bedroom door. I haven't shut it yet because I still have five minutes left before lights out, so I call him.

He pushes his nose through the gap and pads in. Gently, he puts a paw up on my bed.

I pat the doona with my hand. 'Up, come on!'

He jumps up, licks my face and tries to sit on my book. I giggle and pat the end of the bed. 'Go on, sit down there,' I say.

He lies down in a proud dog pose, front paws out and chest up. His white flame is just within scratching reach.

I think of him with those sheep, how he knew exactly what he was doing and how happy Grub the Farmer was with his work.

'Seriously, Zoom,' I say while I scratch, 'You are the world's best dog.'

THE END

About the author

Deb Fitzpatrick is the author of ten books. Her novels have received awards in Australia, been published in the US and optioned for film. Deb has a Master of Arts from UWA and loves using stories from real life in her writing. She regularly teaches creative writing to people of all ages. In her early writing days, Deb did all manner of jobs to fund her writing including making bad coffee, cleaning houses, supervising university exams, and, most pleasantly, helping kids cross the road safely as a crosswalk attendant, or 'lollipop lady'. She lived for several years in the cloudforest of Costa Rica and still pretends to speak some Spanish. Deb loves bushwalking and shares her life with a lovely family and their kelpie, who is absolutely not a failed sheepdog.

Acknowledgements

Kelpie Chaos is a book with a veritable village behind it. It started life as a picture book, and I was very grateful to receive early feedback from talented author-illustrators Briony Stewart and Karen Blair, whose suggestions were crucial in honing the character of Zoom and the journey he took. Dianne Wolfer then suggested I write the story as a novel, and that is when things fell into place for this kelpie. I can't thank Di enough for her input throughout, some of which came at a time of personal struggle, and all of which was artistically generous.

The first draft of this book was written at Minderoo Station, thanks to the generous support of Minderoo Foundation's Artist Fund. I was graciously hosted by station managers Katrina and Hamish (Hamish is the real 'Grub'; thank you for allowing me to abscond with your nickname, Hamish!). I spent three glorious weeks beside the Ashburton River under big starry skies, surrounded by the welcoming staff of this working cattle station; thank you to everyone at Minderoo for this experience.

My agent, Clive Newman, read many iterations of Zoom's story and I'm so grateful for his support and feedback.

Huge thanks to Fremantle Press children's publisher Cate Sutherland, for always seeing what I can't, and so artfully suggesting what's needed. Cate's patience and skill are woven throughout this book. Thank you, Cate.

To my family, especially Stew: thank you. Most of all, thanks and love go to our beautiful kelpie, Louie, who does indeed have a small white flame on his chest.